The kite and children flew out of the window and rose into the air. The apple tree in the yard got smaller and smaller. Caroline looked down and saw the lights of Brooklyn far below.

They were flying over Ocean Parkway. The kite went so fast that Paul and Caroline could hear the wind whistling past them. After a while the kite flew more slowly. It was coming down.

"That's water down there!" Paul said.

The kite swooped lower. A splash of salty spray dashed over Caroline. "Watch out!"

Also by Ruth Chew

MAGIC IN THE PARK

NO SUCH THING AS A WITCH

THE TROUBLE WITH MAGIC

THE WEDNESDAY WITCH

WHAT THE WITCH LEFT

THE WITCH AT THE WINDOW

WITCH'S BROOM

THE WOULD-BE WITCH

THREE ADVENTURE TALES
(AN EBOOK OMNIBUS):
LAST CHANCE FOR MAGIC
MAGIC OF THE BLACK MIRROR
SUMMER MAGIC

THREE SHRINKING TALES
(AN EBOOK OMNIBUS):
DO-IT-YOURSELF MAGIC
EARTHSTAR MAGIC
MOSTLY MAGIC

THREE WISHING TALES
(AN EBOOK OMNIBUS):
THE MAGIC COIN
THE MAGIC CAVE
THE WISHING TREE

THREE WITCH TALES
(AN EBOOK OMNIBUS):
THE WITCH'S BUTTONS
WITCH'S CAT
THE WITCH'S GARDEN

RUTH CHEW

SECONDHAND MAGIC

with illustrations by the author

A STEPPING STONE BOOK™

Random House New York

Random House and the colophon are registered trademarks and A Stepping Stone Book and the colophon are trademarks of Penguin Random House LLC.

Visit us on the Web!
SteppingStonesBooks.com
randomhousekids.com

Educators and librarians, for a variety of teaching tools, visit us at RHTeachersLibrarians.com

Library of Congress Cataloging-in-Publication Data is available upon request.

ISBN 978-0-449-81582-3 (pbk)

Printed in the United States of America
10 9 8 7 6 5 4 3 2 1
First Random House Edition

This book has been officially leveled by using the F&P Text Level Gradient™ Leveling System.

For my nephew,
Pierre-Yves Chew

SECONDHAND MAGIC

"What's that funny thing up there, Caroline?" Paul Henderson pointed to the top of a tall tree.

Paul and his sister were walking around Lookout Mountain in Prospect Park.

Caroline stared at the tree. Something deep blue and bright orange was fluttering on one of the branches. "I think it's a kite."

"It sure must be a big one." Paul left the path and started down the hill.

Caroline went after him. "Watch out for that poison ivy!"

They made a wide circle around a patch of shiny green leaves. Caroline stopped to sniff the yellow blossoms of a honeysuckle vine. She looked up to see Paul standing under the tall tree.

The branches were close together. It looked like an easy tree to climb. By the time Caroline got to it, Paul was on the fourth branch.

"Paul, come down here!" she yelled. "That's a pine tree! Remember Dad said they're not safe to climb."

"You just aren't good at climbing." Paul went higher in the tree.

Caroline was two years older than Paul. And her legs were longer. She could climb up trees even better than he could. But she lost her nerve when she had to come down. Now she sat on the ground under the tree to watch Paul.

He climbed up four more branches. "It's hot up here. I'm sweating." Paul rubbed his hands on the seat of his pants. "This tree is oozing sap. I'm getting sticky."

"Then why don't you come down?" Caroline asked.

Paul looked up at the blue and orange thing. It flapped in the wind. "It's a kite, all right. And it's shaped like a bird." He started up again.

Crack! A branch snapped under his foot. Paul threw his arms around the trunk of the tree.

Caroline jumped to her feet. "Paul, come down!"

Paul looked down at her. Then he looked up at the kite. "I'm more than halfway there." He pulled himself onto the next branch.

Caroline stood quite still under the pine tree. She was afraid if she moved Paul might look down and get dizzy. Secretly she wanted him to get the kite. And that made her feel it would be her fault if anything happened to her brother.

Paul was high in the tree now.

Caroline saw him reach up and touch the kite. It gave a little twist and a shake.

"Hold still!" Paul said.

At once the kite stopped moving.

Paul pulled the prickly pine branches away from it. Soon the kite was free.

"This kite's bigger than I am," Paul said. "I don't know how I'm going to carry it down."

"Why don't you just drop it?" Caroline said.

Paul let go of the kite. Caroline wondered why the kite didn't bump into the branches as it drifted toward the ground. When Caroline caught it, she was nearly knocked off her feet.

Paul climbed carefully down the tree.

"It's a beautiful bird! And it's made of

cloth instead of paper." Caroline stroked the big kite. Suddenly she stopped and stared at it.

Paul was on the ground now. "What's the matter?" he asked.

"I know it's silly," Caroline said, "but for a moment I thought it was rubbing its head against my hand."

Paul looked hard at the kite. "It's floppy on one side."

Caroline turned it over. "One of the sticks is broken. No wonder it was flapping so much."

"Let's take it home. Maybe we can glue it," Paul said.

Caroline picked up the head of the cloth bird. Paul held on to the tail. Together they carried the big kite up the hill to the path.

"It's no fun to go back the same way we came," Paul said. "Let's walk across the top of Lookout Mountain."

They followed the path around the hill. At the top of some steps they came to a wide stone walk.

Paul pointed to a bench. "Let's sit down for a while. I'm tired."

As Paul and Caroline walked toward the bench, they saw that there was already someone there. A little man with a scraggly gray beard and shaggy eyebrows was lying on the bench. His eyes were closed, and he was smiling as if he were having a happy dream. The children saw that he had folded up a heavy overcoat and was using it as a pillow.

"Why does he have an overcoat with him in this weather?" Paul asked.

Caroline put her finger to her lips. "Sh-sh!"

The little man woke up. He sat up and rubbed his eyes.

The kite tugged at Caroline's hands. A gust of wind must have caught it, she thought. Caroline held tight to the orange head to keep it from being yanked away. The kite skimmed along the stone walk. Caroline had to run to keep up with it.

"Slow down, Caroline!" Paul raced after her, holding on to the tail of the kite.

Caroline's feet were barely touching the walk now. "Hang on, Paul!" she yelled.

The broken kite flapped in the wind.

But it kept flying just above the stone walk. It crossed the top of Lookout Mountain and started down the other side.

The kite pulled Caroline and Paul down some steps. Then it began to go slower and slower. At last it gave a little shake and went limp.

"The wind must have died down," Caroline said.

"My arms ache." Paul put the kite down. "Why were you running, Caroline? Were you afraid of that man?"

"I was trying to keep the kite from blowing away," Caroline told him.

"Wow!" Paul said. "If the kite flies like this when it's broken, I wonder what it will do after we mend it."

3

"Where's the glue, Mom?" Paul finished his milk and got up from the lunch table.

"We're out of it," Mrs. Henderson said. "What do you want it for?"

"One of the sticks on the kite we found is broken, Mother," Caroline told her. "Paul and I were going to glue it."

"I was wondering why anybody would leave a kite like that in the park," Mrs. Henderson said. "It's made of silk. I was worried that someone might be looking for it. You can buy some glue at Kenny's."

"They're sure to have it," Caroline said.

Mrs. Henderson laughed. "They seem to have everything in that little store. I've seen things there nobody else sells anymore." She went to get her handbag and fished out two quarters. "This ought to be enough for a tube of glue. Try not to lose it, Caroline."

Paul and Caroline left the house and walked two blocks down Church Avenue to a little variety store on the corner. Inside, Mrs. Kenny was busy sorting a pile of notebooks.

The children walked to the back of the store where the toys were. Paul looked at a model airplane. Caroline found a tiny armchair that would be just right for her dollhouse.

Mrs. Kenny came over to Paul and Caroline. "What are you two looking for today?"

"Glue," Caroline told her.

"We just got in an order this morning," Mrs. Kenny said. "I haven't unpacked it yet. I'll go and get you a tube." She went down a stairway to the basement.

Caroline put down the little chair and walked toward the front of the store. The young woman behind the cash register was Madeline, Mrs. Kenny's daughter. "Hello, Caroline," she said. "I didn't expect to see you and Paul till you needed school supplies in the fall."

Just as Paul was walking past the counter where books of needles and spools of thread were stacked, a small dog rushed past him. A lady came chasing after it. She bumped into Paul. He slipped and knocked over a pile of cards of embroidery thread.

The little dog grabbed a card with his teeth. He dashed out of the store. The lady ran after him.

When Mrs. Kenny came up from the basement, she saw Paul and Caroline picking up the cards of thread. "Oh, dear! Haven't I told you children not to mess up the stock?"

"It wasn't their fault," Madeline told her mother. "Mrs. Baker's dog was running wild."

Just then Mrs. Baker came back into the store. She was holding her dog in her arms. "I'm sorry, Mrs. Kenny." Mrs. Baker put the card of orange thread on the counter.

Mrs. Kenny looked at it. "I can't sell this now. Your dog has chewed the card."

Mrs. Baker took the card of thread to the cash register and paid for it. "I don't need embroidery thread," she said. "Have fun with it, dear." She handed the card to Caroline and walked out of the store.

Mrs. Kenny put a tube of glue on the counter beside the cash register. Caroline took out her two quarters.

"The price has gone up to seventy-nine cents," Madeline said.

"Mother only gave us fifty cents." Caroline turned to go out of the store.

"Wait a minute, Caroline. I've got something here that might help you." Madeline took a tiny blue tube off the shelf behind the cash register and handed it to Caroline.

Caroline put the quarters on the counter.

Mrs. Kenny's daughter shook her head. "It's a present," she said. "Let me know how it works, and maybe I'll order some."

When they got home, Caroline gave her mother the two quarters. "Glue has gone up to seventy-nine cents."

"Everything costs three times what it used to," Mrs. Henderson said.

"Mrs. Kenny's daughter gave Caroline a free sample," Paul said.

Mrs. Henderson smiled. "That was nice of her. I hope you thanked her, Caroline."

Paul started up the stairs. "Come on, Caroline. Let's glue the kite stick."

Caroline picked up yesterday's newspaper. She took it up to her room and spread it on the floor. "Just in case we spill the glue." She laid the kite on the newspaper and took the little blue tube out of her pocket.

Caroline read the label. "Magic glue. Works instantly."

"Give it to me." Paul put a shining drop of glue on the broken ends of the kite stick.

Caroline pushed the ends together. At once the stick was in one piece. They couldn't even see the crack where it had been broken.

The kite gave a little shake and floated up to the ceiling.

Caroline looked up at it. For a moment she couldn't speak. Then she whispered, "Paul, the glue really *is* magic!"

"We'd better get the kite off the ceiling before Mom comes in here." Paul began to tug at a piece of orange string that hung down from the kite. But he couldn't pull the kite down.

Caroline took the card of orange

embroidery thread out of the back pocket of her jeans. Paul tied one end of the thread to the kite string. Then he put a dab of glue on the knot.

While they watched, the knot melted away. The kite string became shiny and silky like the embroidery thread. Together they made one long, strong string. Caroline and Paul both took hold of it and yanked. But still the kite stayed up on the ceiling.

Caroline gave the string a gentle pull. "Beautiful Bird, please come down."

The kite floated down and landed on the bed. Caroline went over and smoothed the orange silk head. "Paul, it wants to be called Bird."

The kite rubbed against Caroline's hand.

"Bird," Paul said, "you've been magic all along. It's not just the glue."

The kite stood up and rested on its

tail. It swung around to face Paul.

"Do you think Bird is a boy or a girl?" Caroline asked.

"A boy, of course," Paul said.

The kite tipped forward, as if to nod.

"I guess you're right." Caroline patted one of the blue wings.

The kite hopped off the bed onto the floor. It hopped all around Caroline. Then it flew to the window and tapped against the pane.

"You're trying to tell us something, Bird," Caroline said. "Do you want to go out?"

The kite tapped on the window again.

"There isn't time to go to the park before supper," Caroline said.

"Why don't we take him out in the yard?" Paul asked.

Paul and Caroline took the kite downstairs. Mrs. Henderson was in the kitchen. "Did you glue your kite?"

"Yes," Caroline said. "We want to see how it flies."

"You'll need more room than that little backyard to get it up in the air," her mother told her. "But at least it will keep you two busy for a while. And I'll know where to find you when it's supper time."

5

Paul and Caroline carried the big kite into the little yard. They leaned it against the fence. Caroline was holding the card of embroidery thread in her hand.

Paul began to unwind it. "What do you suppose we have to do to get Bird to fly?"

Without warning the kite soared up into the air. Paul grabbed the string. He was pulled up after the kite. A moment later Caroline and the card of thread were dragged off the ground.

In almost no time the children were above the roof of their house. They looked down and saw the backyard getting smaller and smaller.

At first Caroline was afraid the string would break. But the silky embroidery thread was very strong. Paul was clinging to it just under the kite. Caroline held on to the card a little below Paul's feet.

"Bird!" Paul yelled. "This string is cutting into my hands."

The kite began to glide down.

"Hurry, Bird," Paul said. "I don't know how much longer I can take this."

"Slide down and stand on my shoulders, Paul," Caroline said. "But don't let go of the string."

Caroline kept her shoulders as level as she could.

Paul inched his way down the string until his sneakers rested on Caroline's shoulders. The kite dropped lower.

"Is this better, Paul?" Caroline asked.

"A little," Paul said. "But it's not exactly easy riding."

It wasn't easy for Caroline either. But the kite was gliding down. In a few moments they landed on the ground. The two children rolled over each other in a heap.

Paul stood up and looked around. "Where are we?"

Caroline got to her feet. "We're in a backyard. But it isn't ours."

"Bird," Paul said, "you brought us to the wrong house!"

"Don't blame Bird," Caroline said. "Lots of houses in Brooklyn look just like ours." She tied a loop in the kite string with the square knot she learned in scouting.

"What are you doing?" Paul asked.

Caroline made another loop a few inches below the first one. "Stick your feet in these. I'll hang on to the card."

The back door of the house opened, and a man came stamping out into the yard.

Paul shoved his feet into the loops Caroline had made and grabbed hold of the string.

Caroline held on to the card. "Up you go, Bird!"

"What do you think you're doing here?" the man said in a rough voice.

"We're flying," Paul told him.

The kite rose in the air, trailing Paul and Caroline after it.

The man rubbed his eyes. Then he shook his head and walked back into the house.

6

"This is great, Caroline!" Paul said. "It's like riding a horse. And these loops are the stirrups."

Caroline looked up at him. "You'd better tell Bird how to find our house. It makes me dizzy to look down."

Paul leaned over to get a view of the ground. "Bird, you're not even over the right street. Do you see that big pear tree?" Paul pointed to it. "Ours is the yard three houses away, the one that has the tree with little green apples on it."

The kite made a soft landing in their own backyard. Both Paul and Caroline touched the ground feet first.

Caroline clapped her hands. "That was wonderful, Bird!"

The big kite tipped over as if to take a bow.

Paul stepped out of his stirrups. Caroline began winding the string around the card. Their father came out of the house into the yard.

"Your mother told me to call you in for supper." Mr. Henderson caught sight of the big kite. "She said you kids found a kite. But I never expected anything like this!" He walked over to get a better look.

"What sort of string is that?"

"It's embroidery thread, Daddy," Caroline told him. "A lady in Kenny's gave it to me."

Mr. Henderson stared at the string. "It's knotted and tangled. And it's too heavy."

"It's the right color for the kite, Dad," Paul said.

His father nodded. "Matches perfectly. Well, maybe a big kite like that can stand a heavy string. You know, kids," he said, "when I was a boy, I used to be pretty good at flying kites. Would you like me to show you how?"

Neither Paul nor Caroline answered him. But Mr. Henderson didn't seem to notice. "Tomorrow's Sunday," he said. "We'll take the kite to the park. But first you'd better get the knots out of that string."

Mrs. Henderson looked out of the

back door. "Supper's getting cold, Jim. What's going on out here?"

Caroline picked up the kite to take it into the house.

"That's too big for you," Mr. Henderson told her. "You'd better let me have it."

Caroline felt the kite stiffen as she handed it to her father. "Please be careful with him, Dad."

"Of course, Caroline," Mr. Henderson said. "Don't you think I know this is no ordinary kite?"

Mr. Henderson carried the kite upstairs. Paul and Caroline followed close behind.

"Why can't I keep him in my room, Dad?" Paul said. "I was the one who found the kite."

His father looked into Paul's room. "That place is a mess. The kite might get torn on one of those pieces of your Erector set. Why don't you put them away?"

"I'm building a crane with a wrecking ball," Paul said. "I haven't decided yet what to use for a ball."

Mr. Henderson took the kite to Caroline's room. "If you clear a space on top of the bookcase, the kite can go there."

"There's more room on the dresser,

Daddy," Caroline said. "Bird could lie down."

Mr. Henderson laughed. "Fine. But remember to get those knots out of the string."

Mrs. Henderson was calling. "Jim! Bring the children down here. Supper will be ruined!"

Mr. Henderson laid the big kite on the dresser. Then they all went down to the dining room.

After supper Paul and Caroline cleared the table and helped their mother load the dishwasher. When the kitchen was all cleaned up, the children went upstairs.

The kite was looking out of the window into the yard. The string was dragging on the floor.

Caroline ran to pick up the string. The kite floated over to the bed and lay down. Caroline patted it.

She used a pin to loosen the knots in

the embroidery thread. It took her a long time to get them out. The thread was frayed and worn when she finished. "It would be awful if it broke when we were flying," she said.

Paul looked at the string. "What did you do with the magic glue?"

Caroline went to get the little blue tube from the top drawer of her desk. She squeezed a drop on each of the worn places.

The string quivered. It moved so fast it seemed to blur before their eyes. When it stopped moving, Paul said, "It looks like a brand-new string!"

Caroline screwed the cap back on the tube and put the glue away in the drawer.

Next morning, right after breakfast, Mr. Henderson said, "Get your kite, kids. We'll go to the park."

Paul and Caroline went upstairs to Caroline's room. The kite was at the window, watching a flock of starlings splashing in the birdbath.

Paul ran over to it. "Bird, please don't do any wild flying when we're out with Dad."

The kite sank down to the floor.

"Promise!" Paul said.

The kite nodded.

"That's a good boy," Paul said. "Today you'll pretend you're not magic at all."

Caroline thought the kite looked sad. She helped Paul carry it downstairs.

Mr. Henderson was waiting by the front door. "You'd better let me hold that. We don't want anything to happen to this wonderful kite."

The kite arched its back. Caroline was afraid that at any minute it would cock its head. She reached over to give a little

warning pinch to one of the beautiful blue wings.

In Prospect Park a fresh breeze stirred the treetops. "It's a perfect day to fly a kite," Mr. Henderson said.

Sunday was a busy day in the park.

The road there was crowded with bicycles and joggers. Horseback riders galloped along the bridle path. There were families with picnic baskets sitting in the grass. A lot of people had brought fishing poles to see what they could catch. And the lake was jammed with rowboats.

Paul and Caroline walked with their father past the big lake and around Lookout Mountain to the Long Meadow. Mr. Henderson carried the kite.

Teen-aged boys were playing softball in the middle of the big field. A lady was pushing a baby in a stroller along the curving walk. Two big spotted dogs chased a yelping spaniel across the grass.

"Look up there." Mr. Henderson pointed to a red kite zigzagging over the meadow. Beyond it Caroline and Paul saw a box kite bobbing up and down.

"We'll show them what a kite can do."

Mr. Henderson held up the big blue and orange kite to catch the breeze.

The wings sagged, and the kite dropped down instead of rising.

"The wind must have died down," Mr. Henderson said. "Never mind. We can get it to fly without the wind." He held the kite in the air and handed the string to Paul. "Run!"

Paul raced around the meadow, pulling the kite behind him. He ran until he was out of breath. When at last he stopped, the kite took a nose-dive into the grass.

Mr. Henderson picked up the kite and turned it over and over.

"That's the wrong way to treat a kite," someone said. "It's sure to make it dizzy."

Caroline looked around. A very small man was standing behind her. Caroline thought she had seen him before. But she couldn't remember where.

The little man had bright green eyes under shaggy eyebrows. His gray hair curled in little feathery tufts over his ears. He had a scraggly beard. And he was carrying a heavy winter coat.

As soon as she saw the coat, Caroline knew where she had seen him. He was the man who was sleeping on the park bench yesterday.

Mr. Henderson stood and looked at the kite. He scratched his head.

Just then a young man on a bicycle came riding along the walk. "Beautiful kite! Would you like me to help you get it up?"

"You mean with your bike?" Mr. Henderson asked. "Great idea! Thank you!" He handed the kite string to the young man and held the kite in the air.

"Oh, my goodness!" the little man with the overcoat said to Caroline. "What will they do next?"

The young man pedaled his bicycle away down the walk. Mr. Henderson let go of the kite. It flew behind the bicycle.

Mr. Henderson smiled. "Now we're getting somewhere!"

The young man went faster and unwound the string. The kite followed him. But it never rose higher than five feet in the air.

Paul walked over to Caroline. "I told Bird not to do any wild flying. So now he won't fly at all. I feel sorry for Dad."

The little man with the overcoat said, "That kite looks just like one I used to have. I didn't think there was another one like it."

Paul stared at the man. "You had a kite like that one?"

The man smoothed his beard. "Well, not quite like that one. *Mine* was a great flyer. It was always flying away from me. And it went so fast! By now it must be a hundred miles from here." He turned to Caroline. "I think it wanted a change." He looked sad. "Perhaps it was bored with me."

Paul and Caroline saw the young man on the bicycle winding up the kite string. He pedaled back to Mr. Henderson and handed him the kite. "There's something wrong with the balance," he said. "Too bad. It's such a handsome kite. Why don't you just hang it on the wall?"

The kite seemed to shiver. Caroline ran over to her father. "Daddy, let's go home."

"I can't see anything wrong with this kite," Mr. Henderson said. "You hold it, Caroline, and I'll run."

Caroline held the kite as high as she could. Mr. Henderson started running.

"Bird," Caroline whispered. "Please be good. Just fly like a regular kite. It would make Daddy happy."

The kite didn't move.

"If you don't fly," Caroline said, "Daddy might hang you over the fireplace for a decoration."

The kite flew up into the air so suddenly that Caroline's feet were pulled off the ground. She let go of the kite and tumbled onto the grass.

In a few moments the kite was high in the sky. Mr. Henderson was still holding on to the string. He walked back to where

Caroline was sitting on the ground. Paul came running over.

Mr. Henderson looked very pleased with himself. "You see, kids," he said, "it's all in knowing how."

The big kite flew high over the meadow. Everybody was looking at it.

"What a beauty! Where did you get it?" a lady asked.

Mr. Henderson held the string with both hands. "My children found it yesterday here in the park."

The little man with the overcoat had been watching the kite swoop across the sky. Now he walked over to Mr. Henderson. "Did I hear you say that kite was found in this park yesterday?"

"Yes, my son and daughter brought it home with them," Mr. Henderson told him.

"It's funny," the little man said, "but I lost a kite just like that one yesterday."

Mr. Henderson looked at Caroline and Paul. "Do you hear that, kids? You know there can't be many kites like this."

"I thought mine was the only one," the man told them. "But my kite was always ready to fly. You had a lot of trouble getting this one up. Maybe it isn't mine."

"Is there any way you could tell yours?" Mr. Henderson asked.

The man reached into the pocket of the overcoat he was carrying. He pulled out a ball of orange string. "Here's the kite string. It broke. My kite would have a short piece of string like this tied to it." He looked at the silky embroidery thread. "This is quite different. I guess it isn't my kite."

Mr. Henderson turned to Caroline. "Didn't you tell me a lady in Kenny's gave you this embroidery thread?"

Caroline couldn't say a word. She nodded her head.

"Paul," Mr. Henderson said, "you found the kite. Was there a short piece of this kind of string on it?"

Paul didn't answer.

Caroline swallowed hard. "Yes,

Daddy, there was," she said in a low voice.

"That settles it. We'll have to give the kite back." Mr. Henderson handed the silken kite string to the little man.

"Thank you." The man with the overcoat began to pull down the kite.

"Come along, kids," Mr. Henderson said. "We'd better go home now."

Paul and Caroline followed their father across the meadow. When they came to Lookout Mountain, Mr. Henderson said, "Never mind. I'll buy you another kite."

"I told the children someone must be looking for that kite," Mrs. Henderson said.

Mr. Henderson took a pretzel from the box in the kitchen cabinet. "We're going to buy another kite."

"Don't bother, Dad," Paul said.

Caroline came into the kitchen. "What's for lunch, Mother?" She wished everybody would stop talking about the kite.

"Stuffed green peppers," Mrs. Henderson said. "Go and wash your hands."

After lunch Caroline and Paul went to Caroline's room.

"If Dad weren't so crazy about kites, we'd still have Bird," Paul said.

"Don't blame Daddy. It was all my fault." Caroline looked as if she were going to cry.

"What do you mean?" Paul asked.

"As long as Bird didn't fly, that man thought he wasn't his kite. And then I went and *made* Bird fly!" Caroline told him.

"The worst part," Paul said, "is that Bird is scared of that spooky little man."

"What makes you think that?" Caroline wanted to know.

"When the man started to wake up yesterday, Bird dragged us across Lookout Mountain. He was afraid the man would see him. Remember he said Bird was always running away from him?"

"I don't want to talk about it anymore." Caroline took a library book off the top of her bookcase. She stretched out on the floor to read it.

Paul went to his room to work with his Erector set.

Caroline spent the rest of the afternoon reading. She tried to forget about the kite. But when she went to bed that night, she kept thinking about it. She thought about the man with the overcoat, too. In spite of what Paul said, Caroline couldn't help liking the little man. It was a long time before she fell asleep.

Some time later in the night she was awakened by a tapping on her window screen. Caroline got out of bed and went to see what was making the noise.

A full moon was high in the sky. Caroline could see something floating in the air just outside her window.

"Bird!" she whispered. "You've come back!" She pushed up the window screen.

The magic kite sailed into the room.

12

"Wake up, Paul," Caroline whispered.

Paul opened his eyes. "What do you want?"

"Get up and put your clothes on," Caroline said. "Bird wants to take us for a ride."

Paul was still half asleep. "Bird?"

Caroline pulled the sheet off him. "Hurry and get dressed. Bird's waiting in my room."

Paul sat up. "How did Bird get in your room?"

"We'll talk later." Caroline ran back to her own room. She slipped into a shirt and blue jeans and put on her sneakers.

The kite was just inside the window.

In the moonlight Caroline saw the embroidery thread hanging down.

Paul came into the room. "If the string didn't break, how did Bird get away from that man?"

"*My* string didn't break. But there was a short piece of orange string tied to the end of it. It was the same kind that broke before." Caroline finished tying two small loops. "Here are your stirrups, Paul."

"The card for the embroidery thread is gone," Paul said. "Why don't you make stirrups for yourself?"

Caroline tied a large loop about four feet below the stirrups. "I can sit in this."

Paul climbed on the window sill to get his feet into the stirrups. "Where shall we go?"

Caroline sat in the big loop as if it were a swing. "Let's leave it up to Bird."

She looked up at the kite. "Take us to a place where we can have fun."

The kite flew out of the window and rose into the air. The apple tree in the yard got smaller and smaller. Caroline looked down and saw the lights of Brooklyn far below.

They were flying over Ocean Parkway. The kite went so fast that Paul and Caroline could hear the wind whistling past them. After a while the kite flew more slowly. It was coming down.

"That's water down there!" Paul said.

The kite swooped lower. A splash of salty spray dashed over Caroline. "Watch out, Bird!"

The kite sailed up into the air, towing Paul and Caroline after it. Then it flew slowly down until their feet touched a sandy beach.

"A perfect landing!" Caroline let go of her swing. She went to stroke the kite's head. "You're getting better all the time, Bird."

The orange silk rubbed against her hand.

13

Paul slipped out of the stirrups and looked around. The white beach gleamed in the moonlight. "Hey, Caroline, there's a boardwalk over there!"

"It's Coney Island," Caroline said. "But it looks different without people."

"Let's go wading." Paul took off his sneakers.

They rolled up their jeans and left their sneakers beside the kite. Then they raced to the edge of the water.

The wet sand felt wonderful between their toes. A wave washed around their ankles.

Caroline and Paul were all alone on the wide beach. The only noise was the pounding of the surf. It seemed strange

not to hear the seagulls screaming overhead. They must be asleep at this time of
night, Caroline thought.

Far out across the water a lighthouse
was flashing. Caroline wondered if there
was anybody awake in it.

Paul and Caroline played tag with the
waves. They ran after each wave as it
pulled back into the ocean. Then they

turned around and raced the next wave to the beach.

"I'm going to build a castle." Caroline sat down on the sand.

Paul got down on his hands and knees. "You've got to have a moat."

Caroline used the wet sand Paul scooped out of his moat to make a square castle with round towers on the corners. Together they built a wall around everything. Caroline showed Paul how to stick little black mussel shells along the wall to make a spiky top.

The castle was almost finished when a wave dashed against the wall. A few seconds later another wave flooded the moat.

Caroline jumped to her feet. "The tide's coming in!"

They ran back along the beach to the place where they had left the kite. There was water everywhere there. Caroline grabbed Paul's hand to pull him higher on the beach.

"What will we tell Mom if we lose our sneakers?" Paul said. "We'd better find them."

"How about Bird?" Caroline said. "I don't think he can swim."

"There he is in the water!" Paul pulled his arm free and ran to the ocean. He fished up an armful of something soft and slimy. "It's not Bird," he said. "Only seaweed."

A big wave knocked Paul down. Caroline waded through the surf to reach him. She tried to pull her brother to his feet. But it was all she could do to keep from falling into the water too.

All at once something lumpy banged against Caroline's shoulder. She grabbed hold of it. A moment later Caroline was dragged out of the water. "Hang on, Paul!" she yelled.

Paul held on to Caroline's ankles. Both children were pulled up into the air.

Caroline saw the big kite flying overhead. It soared up, trailing Paul and Caroline after it.

The kite crossed the beach. It floated down and landed beside a bench on the boardwalk.

The children fell off in a heap. Paul let go of Caroline's ankles. By the light of a street lamp beside the bench, Caroline could see the lumpy bundle she was holding.

It was the four sneakers. They were all rolled up in kite string.

14

The big kite was perched on the arm of
the bench.

Caroline was trying to unwind the
string from around the sneakers. "How
did you do it, Bird?"

"I gave it some help," a voice said.

Now Caroline saw that there was a man lying on the bench. He sat up and turned to look at the children.

Paul stared at him. "You're the man Dad gave the kite to! What are you doing here?"

The little man smoothed his scraggly beard. "I was sleeping," he said, "until the kite woke me. It kept poking me and then flying down to the beach and back. It wouldn't leave me alone until I went down after it."

"How did you know what Bird wanted you to do?" Caroline asked.

"The kite showed me your shoes," the little man said. "The water was nearly up to them. So I picked them up."

"Why didn't you just give them to us?" Paul said.

"You had almost finished that lovely castle. And the water hadn't reached you yet. I didn't want to spoil your fun." He smiled. "Anyway, I wanted to see what the kite would do with the shoes if I rolled them up in the string."

Caroline was still untangling the embroidery thread from the sneakers. "Thank you for helping us. I'm Caroline Henderson. And this is my brother, Paul."

"My name is Clement Ellsworth," the man said. "But I like to be called Clem."

"Why are you in Coney Island?" Paul asked.

"I work here," Clement Ellsworth told him.

Caroline finished unwinding the string. She handed Paul his sneakers and started to put hers on. "Clem, why did Bird bring us here?"

"The kite feels at home in Coney Island," Clement Ellsworth said. "It used to be a beach umbrella."

Paul walked over to stroke the kite.

"How did he get to be a kite?"

"The umbrella was always blowing away. It just wouldn't stay in the sand," Clement Ellsworth said. "One day the woman who owned it got so angry she smashed the umbrella."

"How awful!" Caroline said.

"That's what I thought." Clement Ellsworth stood up and picked up his overcoat from the bench. "I took the broken pieces and made a kite out of them. Now the kite keeps flying away. I guess it's afraid I'll turn it back into an umbrella."

"You must be a wizard," Paul said.

"I used to be," Clement Ellsworth told him. "But I had to give up magic."

"Why?" Caroline asked.

"It got harder and harder to find the right things to work with. The stores don't seem to sell them anymore," Clement Ellsworth said. "You can't even buy a jar of vanishing cream these days."

"You made a magic kite," Caroline pointed out.

"The cloth and wood the kite is made of must have been magic to begin with," the little man said. "I wish I knew a store where you could buy things like that."

15

"What do you need that overcoat for?" Paul said. "It's so warm tonight I don't even mind my clothes being wet."

Clement Ellsworth changed the subject. "Do you like those things?" He pointed to a big merry-go-round on the other side of the boardwalk.

Caroline and Paul raced over to it. The kite flew after them.

Caroline looked up at a carved wooden horse. The curly mane shone in the moonlight. The merry-go-round was still and silent. But it would be fun just to sit on the horse.

Paul was already on a wooden giraffe. He put his arms around its long neck. "Isn't this great?"

Caroline climbed onto the horse. She grabbed the reins.

Clang!

The music started, the wonderful whistling sound of a merry-go-round. The big merry-go-round began to turn, and all the painted animals went up and down.

"Look, Caroline," Paul said. "Clem's running it just for us."

The little man was holding on to a long lever with both hands. He was swaying back and forth in time to the music.

When her horse was up high, Caroline could see all the way across the board-walk and the beach to the ocean. The moonlight on the water seemed to dance. The whirling merry-go-round sent a salty breeze blowing through Caroline's hair.

Paul leaned way over to one side of his giraffe. "Whee!" he said.

The music stopped. Paul got off the giraffe and climbed up on a lion. Caroline stayed on her horse.

Clement Ellsworth pushed the lever forward. The merry-go-round began to turn again, and the music pulled and whistled. Paul and Caroline rode round and round.

Suddenly Caroline saw the kite floating over the boardwalk. "Clem, we'd better go."

"Not yet, Caroline," Paul said. "This is such fun."

"It's late," Caroline told him. "And I don't know how we're going to get home. After all, Bird is Clem's kite."

Clem pulled back the lever. He looked at the kite. "It wants to be with you," he said. "Young people are more fun. The kite would fly away from me at the very first chance."

Paul and Caroline climbed down from the merry-go-round. They saw that the embroidery thread was hanging down from the kite, but the loops were too high for them to reach.

"Bird," Caroline called, "please fly low enough for us to come aboard."

The kite dropped down until the silken string dragged on the boardwalk. Paul stuck his feet in the stirrup loops and held on to the string with both hands. The kite rose higher. Caroline sat in her swing.

Clement Ellsworth watched. "I wondered what those loops were for. That's the strongest string I've ever seen. It must be magic."

"Goodnight, Clem," Caroline said. "Thanks for everything. Maybe we can help you sometime."

Clement Ellsworth waved his hand.

The kite sailed up into the air over Coney Island. Caroline looked down to see the little wizard curl up on the bench. He was using his folded coat as a pillow.

16

"Wake up, Caroline! It's a beautiful day." Mrs. Henderson went to the window and pulled down the screen. "You shouldn't leave your screen open," she said. "Before you know it, this room will be full of flies."

Caroline rolled over and hid her face in her pillow.

Her mother walked to the door. "Get up," she said. "I'm going to clean the house. And I don't want you spending all day indoors with that book. I packed a picnic lunch for you and Paul to take to the park."

Caroline sat up and rubbed her eyes. She looked under her bed. Then she ran down the hall to Paul's room.

He was sitting on the floor trying to get the knots out of his shoelaces.

"Where's Bird?" Caroline asked him.

"I don't know," Paul said. "I thought he was in your room."

"He was under my bed when I went to sleep. But he's not there now." Caroline thought for a minute. "I forgot to close my screen."

"Maybe he went out for a little exercise," Paul said. "Anyway, we don't want Mom to see the kite under your bed when she cleans there. We'll be in enough trouble when she finds those wet clothes in the hamper."

Caroline looked all over the house in case the kite was hiding somewhere.

"Eat your breakfast, Caroline." Her mother took the vacuum cleaner out of the hall closet.

After breakfast Mrs. Henderson

pushed the two children out of the front door. She handed Caroline a shopping bag. "Here's your lunch. Don't leave any trash in the park. And try not to break the thermos bottle."

Paul was carrying a little red plastic boat that his uncle had sent him for his birthday. "I'm going to try this out on the lake."

Paul and Caroline walked the five blocks to the park. They kept looking at the sky to see if the kite was anywhere in sight.

At the park gate Caroline shifted the shopping bag to her other arm. "This is heavy." She stopped to watch a pair of squirrels chase each other up and down a chestnut tree. "I'm worried about Clem. I don't think he has a home."

"Maybe that's why he carries his winter coat around in the summertime,"

Paul said. "Did you notice how lumpy the pockets are? He must have everything he owns in them."

They crossed the road in the park and walked over to the lake. Caroline put the shopping bag on the stone wall by the water. Paul took a spool of button thread out of his pocket and tied one end of the thread to his boat. Then he wound up the motor and put the boat into the water.

Paul let the thread unwind as the boat streaked toward the island in the lake. A duck with a beautiful green head came paddling around the end of the island.

Crash! The duck flew up into the air. The little boat started going in circles.

"Dumb duck!" Paul rolled up the thread and took his boat out of the water. "The rudder's broken. That's the end of the boat trip."

Caroline pulled the tiny tube of magic

glue out of her pocket. "I brought this in case we ran into trouble."

They sat down on the stone wall. Paul held the boat while Caroline squeezed a shining drop of glue onto the rudder. She pushed the two broken parts together. An instant later there was no sign of a crack.

"That's wonderful stuff," they heard someone say.

Paul and Caroline looked up. A small man with gray hair was leaning over them. "I guess you don't know me without my beard."

"Clem!" Caroline said.

17

"Why did you shave off your beard, Clem?" Paul asked.

"I thought it would make me look younger," Clement Ellsworth said.

Clement Ellsworth didn't look any younger without his beard. His eyebrows seemed even shaggier. But now Paul and Caroline could see that his mouth turned up at the corners. And there was a dimple in his chin.

Caroline stood up. "We thought you were in Coney Island, Clem. Why are you wearing your overcoat? Are you cold?"

"I was afraid it would blow away when I was flying on the kite." Clement Ellsworth took off the heavy coat and hung it over his arm.

"You mean you flew here on Bird?" Caroline said. "I've been looking everywhere for him."

Clement Ellsworth smiled. "The kite came to get me. I never thought of flying on it until you two showed me how. That swing of yours is great, Caroline."

Clement Ellsworth put two fingers in his mouth and gave a loud whistle. The kite came flying around the trees on the island. It landed on the lake shore beside Caroline.

Caroline patted the kite's head. "I was worried about you, Bird."

Paul was looking at his boat. "It seems different somehow."

Caroline leaned over to get a close look. "It's more like a real boat now."

Clement Ellsworth felt around in the pockets of his baggy coat. "Here it is! I was sure I still had it." He pulled out a spool of tape. "Hand me your boat, Paul."

"What are you going to do?" Paul gave Clement Ellsworth the little boat.

"It's a surprise." The little man got down on his hands and knees. He held the spool against the boat and started to unroll the tape. A short piece dropped off. Then two more strips of tape fell to the ground.

"The surprise is on me," Clement Ellsworth said. "The person who gave me the tape has a very bad temper. She must have chopped it up in one of her tantrums. No wonder she gave it to me. It's no good anymore."

He looked so disappointed that Caroline felt sorry for him. She picked up the strips. They had once been white, but they were dirty gray now. "There are numbers on this tape," Caroline said. "It looks like measuring tape."

"It used to be," Clement Ellsworth said. He looked at the spool in his hand. "I'd better throw it away."

"Let me have it for a minute, Clem," Caroline said.

Clement Ellsworth handed Caroline the rest of the tape. She put all the pieces in the right order with the spool at one end. Then she took the little blue tube out of her pocket and smeared glue on each of the cut edges.

The pieces of tape shivered like a lot of little snakes. When they stopped wiggling they were all joined together. They looked as if they had never been cut apart.

The tape was white and bright and very, very long. It coiled back into the spool with a snap.

Caroline put the tube of glue away again. She picked up the measuring tape and gave it back to Clement Ellsworth.

Clement Ellsworth held the spool of tape over his head and danced a little jig. "You fixed it, Caroline!"

Paul was looking at his boat. He held the wind-up key in his hand. "That's funny!"

"What's the matter?" Caroline asked.

"I can't find the keyhole," Paul said.

Caroline came over to see. "Maybe I spilled glue on it."

"Let's see what the measuring tape will do now, Paul," Clement Ellsworth said. "Put your boat in the water and hold this against the back." He handed Paul the end of the measuring tape.

"I can't see how that's going to help me find the keyhole," Paul said.

"Try it anyway," Caroline told him.

Paul knelt down and put the little red boat in the water. He held the tape against the back of the boat.

Clement Ellsworth began to measure the boat.

Paul and Caroline couldn't believe their eyes.

As the tape unrolled, the boat got bigger.

The kite was so excited it flew up into

the air. Then it coasted down beside Caroline.

In a few moments the boat was so big that Paul had to stand to hold the tape against it.

Clement Ellsworth stopped measuring. "How's that for size?"

"Great!" Paul said. "It's big enough to hold all of us."

"Let go of the tape," Clement Ellsworth said.

Paul let go.

Snap! The measuring tape coiled back into the spool. Clement Ellsworth put it into a pocket of his overcoat.

"It's just like a real motorboat," Paul said.

"Why don't you get in it?" Clement Ellsworth asked him.

Paul stepped into the boat. He sat down behind the steering wheel.

Caroline picked up the shopping bag and climbed into the front seat beside him. "Get in, Bird. We're going for a ride."

The kite hopped onto the back seat.

"You too, Clem," Caroline said.

Clement Ellsworth got in the back with the kite. "It's a long time since I went for a boat ride," he said.

"What are you waiting for, Paul?" Caroline pointed to the dashboard of the boat. "There's your keyhole."

Paul fitted the wind-up key into the lock on the dashboard. He gave the key a turn, and the motor started.

The propeller was spinning, but the boat wasn't moving.

There was a handle near the steering wheel. Paul yanked it toward him. "Oops!"

The red boat backed up.

Before it could crash against the stone wall, Caroline reached across Paul and shoved the handle forward.

The boat streaked across the lake.

Paul pulled the handle back. The boat slowed down. He pushed the handle forward until the boat went at just the right speed. "I've got the hang of it now."

"Caw! Caw! Caw!" A large black

raven flew off the tallest tree on the island
and circled over the boat.

It was Monday, and not many people
were in the park. Around a bend of the
lake two boys were fishing from the stone
wall. Paul waved to them as the boat
whizzed by.

Farther along a fat lady was trying to
stop her little dog from chasing squirrels.
She didn't even look up as the red motorboat passed her.

Three men from the Parks Department were sawing a dead branch off an old elm tree. They were so busy that they didn't notice the boat.

Caroline dipped her fingers in the lake. The water splashed and sparkled in the sunlight. When they passed the place where the little yellow water lilies grew, a bright blue dragonfly sailed over the front of the boat.

Paul was driving close to the edge of

the lake. A weeping willow tree grew on the bank. The long branches trailed down over the water.

"Isn't this a great place for a picnic?" Caroline said.

Paul turned off the motor. The soft green branches of the tree hung around the boat and shaded it from the sun.

"How about having lunch with us, Clem?" Caroline opened the shopping bag.

"Are you sure you have enough?" Clement Ellsworth asked.

Paul laughed. "Mom always packs enough for an army."

Caroline dug out a plastic bag of sandwiches. She took them out one at a time to see what was in them. "There's peanut butter, cream cheese with nuts in it, and meat loaf."

Paul looked into a brown paper bag.

"Peaches and cherries. What's for dessert?"

Caroline lifted a shoebox out of the bottom of the shopping bag. Clement Ellsworth sniffed the air. "Smells like homemade chocolate chip cookies."

Caroline peeked into the box. "You guessed it, Clem." She opened the thermos bottle and filled three paper cups with icy lemonade.

"Mom always packs extra cups," Paul said. "She's afraid if she doesn't we'll drop a cup on the ground and wash it out in the lake."

When the picnic was over, Caroline threw the crumbs to a flock of ducks. She put all the trash back into the shopping bag to take home. "How about letting me drive the boat for a while, Paul?"

20

Caroline drove the boat twice around the lake. "It's your turn now, Clem." She got in back with the kite. "You seem to like boat rides, Bird."

The kite nodded. It was balanced on its tail, looking around at everything.

Clement Ellsworth took hold of the steering wheel. The boat zoomed across the lake. The wind blew through the little

curls around the wizard's ears and made his eyebrows shaggier than ever. His cheeks were pink, and his green eyes sparkled. "I haven't had so much fun in ages."

"Look over there, Caroline," Paul said. "I thought cars weren't allowed to drive here in the daytime." He pointed to a car coming around a curve of the road through the park.

"That's a police car," Caroline said.

The police car stopped near the edge of the lake. Two policemen got out. One of them caught sight of the red motorboat. "Hey, you!" he yelled to Clement Ellsworth. "Don't you know only rowboats are allowed on this lake?"

Clement Ellsworth pretended not to hear. He drove the boat around a point of land and stopped it under an old iron bridge.

Paul climbed out onto the walk that went under the bridge. He held on to the

boat while Caroline, Clement Ellsworth, and the kite got out. Caroline picked up the shopping bag and brought it along.

"Quick, Clem," Paul said. "Make the boat small again."

Clement Ellsworth took the spool of measuring tape out of his pocket and looked at it. Then he put it away again. He rubbed his chin.

"What's the matter?" Caroline asked.

"I just remembered," the little man said, "the tape only makes things bigger."

"What'll we do?" Caroline asked.

"I don't know," Clement Ellsworth said.

Paul looked out from under the bridge. "That policeman is walking around the lake. He's coming this way."

The wizard felt all the pockets of his overcoat. "I've got something that just might do the trick. Now, where did I put it? Ah, here it is!" He pulled out a little pair of scissors.

Paul looked at them. "They're rusty."

"Someone left them in a pail of water for a month," Clement Ellsworth told him. "It didn't do them any good." He had to use both hands to open the scissors.

Crack! The bolt that held the scissors together snapped. The two halves came apart.

Clement Ellsworth held a half in each

hand. "Oh, dear! Now we really are in trouble. I'm afraid we'll just have to leave the boat and run."

"What will I tell Mom?" Paul said. "It's a new boat."

"We don't have time to worry about that now," Clement Ellsworth said. "Let's get out of here."

"Wait a minute, Clem. Give me the scissors." Caroline took the little blue tube out of her pocket. She squeezed the last drops of glue onto the broken ends of the bolt.

Clement Ellsworth pressed the halves of the scissors together.

Paul stared. "They're not rusty anymore."

Caroline looked at the shining scissors. "They're beautiful!"

"Beauty is as beauty does." Clement Ellsworth began to snip at the motorboat.

Paul and Caroline couldn't see

anything snipped off the boat. But it began to get smaller. Soon it was so small that Clement Ellsworth had to bend down to reach it. He went on snipping. A moment later he could lift it out of the water.

The policeman stepped under the bridge. "I've been looking for you," he said. "You're the man with the motorboat. Where is it?"

Clement Ellsworth put the scissors away. He held up the little red boat. "This is the only boat we have, Officer."

The policeman glared at him. He looked all around. Then he walked out from under the bridge and started to search for the motorboat under all the bushes by the lakeside.

21

Clement Ellsworth gave a little hop and a skip. "There's nothing like magic to make you feel young again. I'm beginning to feel like my old self. Where did you get that glue, Caroline?"

They were walking toward the park gate. Caroline carried the shopping bag. There were too many trees for the kite to fly overhead. It was trying to perch on Caroline's shoulder. But it was bigger than she was.

Paul had the little boat under his arm. "The glue came from Kenny's store," he told Clement Ellsworth. "That's where we got the string too."

"I'd like to see what else they have there," the wizard said.

"Do you want us to take you to the store, Clem?" Caroline asked.

"That would be wonderful. Can we go now?" Clement Ellsworth reached into a pocket of his overcoat. "That kite's much too big for you to carry around, Caroline." He lifted the kite off her shoulder.

Snip! Snip! Snip!

Before Caroline or Paul knew what was happening, Clement Ellsworth had used the magic scissors. The kite was no bigger than a butterfly. The string was just a tiny coil of thread.

Clement Ellsworth put the kite into an overcoat pocket. "It's safe now," he said. "Let's go to Kenny's. I'll race you to the gate." He started to run.

Paul and Caroline looked at each other.

"He's back to his old self, all right," Paul said. "And everybody knows you can't trust a wizard."

Caroline clenched her fists. "I was getting to like him a lot. Now I'm sorry I ever mended his broken-down, second-hand magic. Do you think Bird has enough air in that pocket?"

"I don't know," Paul said. "But I'm sure he hates being stuffed in there. No wonder Bird was always running away. Clem must have been doing all sorts of awful things to him."

Clement Ellsworth stopped running.

He looked around. "I guess you don't want to race," he said. "But come along. And don't forget your things."

"We'd better stay close to him," Caroline whispered.

"Why?" Paul asked her.

"Because we have to get that overcoat away from him. It's the only way we'll get Bird back." Caroline started to walk after the wizard.

22

Paul and Caroline followed Clement Ellsworth out of the park. They walked down Ocean Parkway to Church Avenue.

When they came to Kenny's variety store, Clement Ellsworth looked into the plate glass window. "I haven't seen a teakettle like that in years!" He rubbed his hands together. "Has anyone ever told you what happens when one of those starts to boil exactly at midnight?"

Caroline nudged Paul. "As soon as I get a chance, I'll grab his coat and run," she whispered.

"If you don't, I will," Paul said.

The wizard walked into the store. The two children went after him.

Mrs. Kenny's daughter, Madeline, was behind the cash register near the front door. "Hello, Caroline. Did you and Paul try that glue?"

"Yes," Caroline told her. "Thank you for giving it to me. It's wonderful stuff."

"Do you have another tube?" Paul asked.

"That was the only sample the salesman gave me," Madeline said. "It's very expensive. But if your mother wants a tube, I can order one for her."

"How much does it cost?" Caroline asked.

"Seven dollars," Madeline said.

Paul looked at Caroline. "You know Mom wouldn't want to pay that."

"I told the salesman I couldn't sell it at that price." Madeline turned to Clement Ellsworth. "Can I help you?"

"I'd like to see the old-time teakettle you have in the window," the wizard said.

He laid his overcoat on the counter beside the cash register.

Caroline reached for it. Before she could get her hands on the coat, Madeline picked it up and handed it back to Clement Ellsworth.

"I have to keep the counter for merchandise," Madeline said. "Now, are you *sure* you want to buy that teakettle? It's the only one we have. And it will be a lot of trouble to take it out of the window."

"What's the price of the kettle?" Clement Ellsworth asked.

"Fifteen dollars," Madeline told him. "We have some nice whistling kettles that are cheaper."

Mrs. Kenny walked over. "Come," she said, "I'll show them to you." She led the way to a shelf on one side of the little store.

Clement Ellsworth looked at each kettle on the shelf. Caroline and Paul stood beside him. The coat was right next to them. Paul got ready to yank it off the wizard's arm.

Clement Ellsworth shifted the over-coat to his other arm. "These kettles are

not quite what I had in mind. If it's all right with you, I'd like to look around the store."

"Go right ahead." Mrs. Kenny went to help a lady who wanted to buy a rubber floor mat.

Clement Ellsworth walked up and down the aisles. He looked at all the things on the shelves and counters. Paul and Caroline followed right behind him. "Wonderful place!" the wizard said. "I've known a pink bathmat like that one over there to come in mighty handy."

"Would you like to try on one of the funny party hats?" Caroline asked him. He'd have to put down his coat to try on a hat, she thought.

The little man shook his head. "I don't see a hat I like."

Suddenly Clement Ellsworth caught sight of something. "Oh, my!" he said.

"Those look as if they just might fit me."
He sounded very excited. "Here, Caroline, hold this for me, please." He handed
her his overcoat and ran to the back of
the store.

23

"Come on," Paul whispered. "Let's get out of here."

Caroline had the shopping bag handles looped over one arm. She held the overcoat with both hands.

Paul yanked at the coat. "What are you waiting for? Now's our chance. Run!"

"I can't," Caroline said.

Clement Ellsworth was trying on a pair of roller skates with big red clamps on them. His green eyes shone. "They fit! They really fit!"

"They're a real bargain at twelve dollars," Mrs. Kenny told him.

The wizard unstrapped the skates and put them back on the counter. He walked

over to Paul and Caroline. "I don't even have seven dollars to pay for a tube of glue. I'll just have to make some money." He took his overcoat from Caroline and went to the door of the shop.

Caroline and Paul walked out after him.

"Thank you for lunch," Clement Ellsworth said. "I have to go now."

"What about Bird?" Caroline asked. "Aren't you going to measure him back to his right size?"

"The kite is much safer this way," Clement Ellsworth said. "When I want it for something I can always make it bigger. Thanks again for everything. Good-bye." He walked away down Church Avenue toward the subway station.

"He seems to have forgotten that he gave Bird to us." Paul kicked a gum wrapper into the gutter. "But why did you have to go and lose your nerve, Caroline? We could have had Bird, and the magic scissors, and the measuring tape, everything."

"I didn't lose my nerve," Caroline said.

"Then why didn't you run off with Clem's coat when you had the chance?" Paul wanted to know.

"Maybe I could have sneaked Clem's overcoat when he wasn't looking," Caroline said. "But it was different when he gave it to me to keep for him."

Paul thought about this. "You mean you couldn't steal from him when he trusted you."

Caroline swung the shopping bag. "I'm tired of carrying this around. Let's go home, Paul."

When they reached their house, Caroline rang the bell.

Mrs. Henderson opened the door. "How was the picnic?" she asked.

"Great." Caroline handed her mother the shopping bag.

Mrs. Henderson caught sight of the little red boat Paul was carrying. "Is that the boat Uncle George gave you?" She bent over to take a closer look. "I had no idea it was so nicely made. I hope you're careful with it, Paul."

Caroline and Paul walked into the front hall. It was clean and tidy and smelled of furniture polish.

"The house looks nice," Caroline said.

Mrs. Henderson smiled. "Let's see if you can keep it that way at least until Daddy comes home. Put your boat away in your room, Paul." She walked toward the kitchen. "Caroline, give Paul a book to keep him quiet."

24

It was almost suppertime when Mrs. Henderson went upstairs to look for Paul and Caroline. She found them in Caroline's room. They were busy cutting out squares of red blotting paper.

Mrs. Henderson looked at all the little

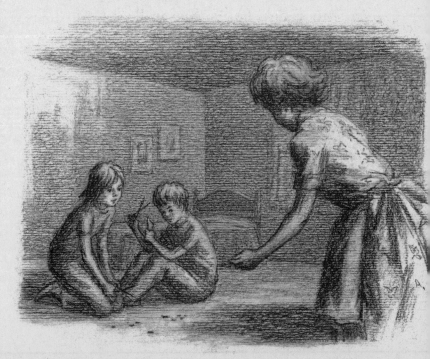

red snippets on the floor. "What are you two up to? Daddy's downstairs with a surprise for you."

"We're making stair treads for Caroline's dollhouse," Paul said.

The children followed their mother downstairs. Mr. Henderson was waiting for them in the front hall. "I bought you a kite, kids."

"Thanks, Dad," Paul said.

"You didn't have to do that, Daddy." Caroline gave her father a hug.

"I want you to take good care of this kite," Mr. Henderson said. "It was very expensive."

Mrs. Henderson turned to look at him. "Expensive, Jim? What did you pay for that kite?"

"Seven dollars."

"Seven dollars!"

"This one is worth every penny of it,"

Mr. Henderson said. "It's a terrific kite, even bigger than the one the kids found."

"Where did you get it?"

"I bought it from a man in the subway station," Mr. Henderson said.

"Where is it, Dad?" Paul asked.

"In the living room," his father said. "Go take a look at it."

Paul and Caroline went into the living room. A blue and orange kite was lying on the coffee table. It was shaped like a bird. As soon as the children stepped through the door, the kite tipped up until it was resting on its tail.

Caroline ran over to it. "Oh, Bird! Is it really you?"

The kite rubbed its orange head against her shoulder.

Paul stared at the kite. "You're bigger than you were."

"Maybe Clem was in a rush to measure him back to size." Caroline stroked one of the deep blue wings.

"We were wrong about Clem," Paul said. "He wasn't trying to take Bird away from us after all."

"He fixed it so Mother and Daddy will let us keep Bird." Caroline patted the orange head of the kite. "I won't have to hide him under my bed now."

"But don't you think it's funny that Dad didn't say anything about Clem?" Paul said.

"Clem looks different without his beard," Caroline reminded him. "Daddy didn't know him."

Paul sat down on the floor to unroll the kite string. "I'm sorry I ever thought those mean things about Clem."

"I wish we could thank him," Caroline said.

Paul looked at the string. "The loops are all in place. Bird is all set to fly. Maybe he knows where we can find Clem."

The big kite nodded.

"Paul," Caroline whispered. "Clem has enough money now to buy the magic glue."

"Yes," Paul said. "And he can mend anything he wants to. I wonder what else he has in the pockets of that old coat."

Let the magic continue. . . .

Here's a sneak peek
at another tale
by Ruth Chew!

The
WEDNESDAY
WITCH

Mischief

"Now don't let any stranger into the house, Mary Jane," said Mrs. Brooks. "I'm going to the supermarket. If the doorbell rings, look through the peep hole first to see who is there. If it's someone you don't know, don't open the door. And don't get into mischief while I'm gone."

Mary Jane watched her mother walk down the tree-lined Brooklyn street. As soon as Mrs. Brooks turned the corner, Mary Jane ran upstairs.

Today she would have plenty of time to go through all the things on her mother's dressing table. Mary Jane wouldn't dare touch them when her mother was around. But now she could even pick them up and try them out. There were so many things—tiny nail scissors, jars of face cream, a pink satin ribbon, three lipsticks, a big box of bath powder, an eyebrow pencil, a magnifying mirror, and—right in the middle, sparkling like a big jewel— a new bottle of perfume. It was called "Mischief."

Mary Jane twisted the stopper and slowly pulled it out of the bottle. At once the room was filled with a strange, exciting smell.

The doorbell rang. Mary Jane ran downstairs, and was about to open the door. Then she remembered what her mother had said. "Before you open the door, look through the peep hole." But the peep hole was high up on the door. So she went to get a dining room chair to stand on. The doorbell rang again.

Mary Jane was pushing the chair against the door when the brass door knocker banged loudly. Whoever was outside must be very impatient, Mary Jane thought. She climbed up on the chair. The door knocker banged again.

A harsh voice screamed, "Is anybody home?"

Mary Jane put one eye to the peep hole and looked out. On the doorstep stood a short fat woman wearing a tall pointed hat. She had a vacuum cleaner with her, the kind that looks like a large jug. A skinny black cat with big yellow eyes and a ragged tail sat on top of the vacuum cleaner. And the hose to the vacuum cleaner was coiled around the fat woman's neck like a big snake.

Mary Jane tried to make her voice sound deep and growly. "Who are you?"

"I want to show you a vacuum cleaner," said the woman. She seemed to be trying to make her voice low and sweet, but it sounded like a scratchy whisper. "It's a lovely vacuum cleaner. I will clean your house for you."

She looked so funny standing there in her long black dress and her pointy hat that Mary Jane could not help teasing. "You can't fool me," she said in the same deep voice. "You are a wicked witch! Go away!"

With a loud click Mary Jane shut the peep hole. Then, ever so quietly, she opened it again and looked out. She saw the short fat woman shake her fist, stamp her foot, and then sit down on the vacuum cleaner. The woman held the metal wand in front of her and shouted, "Home, James!"

The vacuum cleaner rose into the air with the witch. Mary Jane jumped off the chair and opened the door. She saw the witch sail higher and higher, over the tree-tops, higher than the apartment building on the corner. Mary Jane watched until the witch sailed away out of sight.

"Meow." It was the thin black cat, sitting sadly on the doorstep.

The witch must have forgotten her cat, thought Mary Jane, or perhaps she is trying to trick me.

"Meow," said the cat again. Then, to Mary Jane's surprise, it said, "I'm hungry."

Mary Jane couldn't help feeling sorry for the skinny cat. "There's some tuna fish left over from lunch," she said. "Would you like that?"

"I don't know," said the cat. "I've never had fish. All the witch feeds me is toads—when she remembers to feed me at all. And she has a pot of witch's brew that she thinks is delicious, but I can't stand it."

"What's your name, cat?"

"The witch calls me 'Hey, you!'"

"Oh, you poor thing!" cried Mary Jane, and she scooped up the cat. It was so light! Mary Jane could feel all the bones under the scraggly fur. She carried the cat into the house and shut the door.

Mary Jane fed the cat in the kitchen. The cat ate the tuna fish hungrily but daintily. Then she drank a bowl full of milk. When she had finished she washed her face, smoothed her whiskers, and licked herself all over.

Soon the black fur was smooth and shining. "You need a ribbon!

There is a pink satin one that came on Mother's perfume."

Mary Jane carried the cat upstairs to her mother's bedroom and tied the ribbon in a bow around the cat's neck. "Just see yourself, cat." Mary Jane put her on the dressing table in front of the mirror.

The cat looked at her-self with pride. "The witch would hardly know me."

"Tell me about the witch," begged Mary Jane. "What was she doing here?"

"It's Wednesday, and she's a Wednesday Witch."

"What's a Wednesday Witch?"

"Her magic is at its best on Wednesday. The rest of the week she works on her spells. On Wednesday she comes out of her cave and looks for mischief. She said she smelled mischief on your street today."

"Oh," said Mary Jane. "I'd better put Mother's perfume away." She put the stopper in the bottle and put the bottle in its place. She was none too soon.

Mary Jane heard the sound of a key in the front door. She picked up the cat and ran downstairs. Her mother came puffing into the house with two large bags of groceries.

When Mrs. Brooks saw the cat, she put the bags on the floor. "Mary Jane, I've told you not to bring cats into the house. Take it back where it belongs."

Mary Jane watched her mother put away the groceries. She was glad to see three new cans of tuna fish.

Mary Jane's mother was folding the empty grocery bags. "Oh, dear, I'll never get the house tidy before your father comes home. Here, put the bags away."

"I can't take the cat back, Mother."

Mary Jane took the bags. "It's a witch's cat. She flew away on a vacuum cleaner, and left the cat here."

"Vacuum cleaner!" said Mary Jane's mother. "Mary Jane, could you vacuum the rug?"

While Mary Jane went to get the vacuum cleaner, Mrs. Brooks went into the living room with a dustcloth, and the cat followed her. Mrs. Brooks was about to dust a vase when she saw the cat jump to the mantelpiece and walk softly to the tall silver candlestick beside the clock. The cat dusted it carefully with her tail and swished away the dust around it.

Moving to the clock she dusted that too. She gave a few expert flicks of her tail to the candlestick on the other side of the clock and leaped to the bookcase to dust a little china lady and a glass bowl. Mrs. Brooks put down the vase. The cat walked over to it, swished her tail up and around the vase, and jumped to the floor. Then she looked at Mary Jane's mother with big sad eyes.

Dusting was not something Mrs. Brooks enjoyed. This cat seemed to love it. For a long time Mary Jane's mother just stood there. At last she said, "Are you *sure* that cat doesn't belong to anyone?"

By this time Mary Jane was running the vacuum cleaner. She had to shout to make herself heard over the sound of the motor. "Oh, she belongs to the witch."

Mrs. Brooks turned off the vacuum cleaner. "Mary Jane, I've told you so many times not to make up stories. Does the cat have a name?"

"The witch calls her 'Hey, you!'"

After a moment's thought Mary Jane's mother announced, "I'm going to call her 'Cinders' because she does the work like Cinderella. Poor thing, she is much too thin."